World War I
In Flanders Fields

Dorothy Alexander Sugarman

Associate Editor
Torrey Maloof

Editor
Wendy Conklin, M.A.

Editorial Director
Dona Herweck Rice

Editor-in-Chief
Sharon Coan, M.S.Ed.

Editorial Manager
Gisela Lee, M.A.

Publisher
Rachelle Cracchiolo, M.S.Ed.

Creative Director
Lee Aucoin

Illustration Manager/Designer
Timothy J. Bradley

Cover Designer
Lesley Palmer

Cover Art
Corbis
Kryzsztof Slvsarczyk/Shutterstock, Inc.
The Library of Congress

Teacher Created Materials
5301 Oceanus Drive
Huntington Beach, CA 92649
http://www.tcmpub.com
ISBN 978-1-4333-0551-1
© 2009 Teacher Created Materials, Inc.
Reprinted 2011
Printed in China

World War I:
In Flanders Fields

Story Summary

Dr. John McCrae is a Canadian doctor who enlists to run a field hospital during WWI. His dedication to his country inspires his niece, Jillian, and she enlists to serve as a nurse at his hospital. The hospital staff, including a dedicated lieutenant named Alexis, struggles to keep up with the hospital's demands. After helping and comforting a wounded soldier, Alexis leaves to get some sleep in the dugout. Unfortunately, the next morning, he is struck and killed by a German shell while trying to help another wounded soldier. Grieving the loss of Alexis, Dr. McCrae writes the famous poem, "In Flanders Fields," and he and his staff contemplate "the war to end all wars."

Tips for Performing Reader's Theater

Adapted from Aaron Shepard

- Don't let your script hide your face. If you can't see the audience, your script is too high.

- Look up often when you speak. Don't just look at your script.

- Talk slowly so the audience knows what you are saying.

- Talk loudly so everyone can hear you.

- Talk with feelings. If the character is sad, let your voice be sad. If the character is surprised, let your voice be surprised.

- Stand up straight. Keep your hands and feet still.

- Remember that even when you are not talking, you are still your character.

Tips for Performing
Reader's Theater *(cont.)*

- If the audience laughs, wait for them to stop before you speak again.

- If someone in the audience talks, don't pay attention.

- If someone walks into the room, don't pay attention.

- If you make a mistake, pretend it was right.

- If you drop something, try to leave it where it is until the audience is looking somewhere else.

- If a reader forgets to read his or her part, see if you can read the part instead, make something up, or just skip over it. Don't whisper to the reader!

World War I:
In Flanders Fields

Characters

Alexis Helmer	**Nurse Hathaway**
Cyril Allinson	Dr. John McCrae
Robert Smith	**Nurse Jillian**

Setting

This reader's theater takes place in various hospitals during World War I. In the beginning, the scene is set at Royal Victoria Hospital in Montreal, Canada. Then, the action moves to a field hospital in Ypres, Belgium. There is constant gunfire and shells exploding outside, but occasionally the area quiets, and the staff enjoys the birds who sing in Flanders Field, a cemetery full of white crosses.

Act 1

Alexis Helmer: You learn to love the men you fight side by side with during a time of war. Your life depends on them, and their lives depend on you. They become your family. That's the way I felt about Dr. John McCrae, the leader of our battalion.

Cyril Allinson: I'm sure Dr. McCrae's nightmares still haunt him. My nightmares still haunt me. I was the Sergeant Major in his battalion and worked alongside Dr. McCrae and Lieutenant Alexis Helmer during those terrible days. Dr. McCrae referred to them as the "17 days in Hades."

Alexis Helmer: Dr. McCrae and I are both Canadian, and we both love our country. What we went through together was unbearable. What we saw was unimaginable, and what we needed to do every day was impossible. I would have done anything for Dr. McCrae.

Cyril Allinson: I know that going to war was not an easy decision for Dr. McCrae. He is a doctor. He is a man of healing. But, he felt he owed it to his country.

Robert Smith: I met Dr. McCrae because I was one of the thousands of wounded people he treated during the war.

Nurse Hathaway: I worked as a nurse in that field hospital. I know how upset Dr. McCrae became during our time there. He certainly had good reasons.

Robert Smith: We told one another everything during those days because we didn't know how long we would live, and we all craved close human contact. No one wants to be forgotten, and no one wants to die alone.

Nurse Hathaway: I always wondered if Dr. McCrae was sorry that he made the decision to enlist. He told me how much he dreaded telling his niece, Jillian, that he had decided to do so. He wasn't sure what to say to her. He never expected the reaction he got.

Dr. John McCrae: I will never forget the day I told Jillian I was going to join the war effort. I knew she would be worried and upset by my decision, but believe me, I didn't expect what happened next. Jillian Turner was not just my niece. She worked next to me every day as a nurse at the Royal Victoria Hospital in Montreal, Canada.

Nurse Jillian: I remember my uncle running up to me in the hospital on that day. I could see he was terribly worried about something.

Dr. John McCrae: She knew Europe was on the brink of disaster, but in her mind, what did that have to do with Canada? What did that have to do with us?

Nurse Jillian: I had read the headlines, and I had a lot of questions for him. What he said changed both of our lives forever. Come with me back in time and hear this story for yourself.

Dr. John McCrae: I must speak with you now, Jillian. There is a matter of grave urgency that is bound to change the world as we know it. Have you read the newspaper headlines today? Do you have any idea of what's happening?

Nurse Jillian: I saw the newspaper headlines, Uncle. They say that a "Great War" is beginning in Europe because of the "shot heard around the world." I know that the shot they are referring to is the one that killed Archduke Franz Ferdinand. But I must tell you, I don't understand. How could the death of one man lead to a war?

Dr. John McCrae: That's a good question, my dear. There is a great and terrible rivalry between the countries in Europe. Archduke Franz Ferdinand was next in line to be the king of Austro-Hungary. He was shot and killed during his visit to Serbia. Right away, the Austrians blamed his death on the Serbian government. But, I think it was an excuse. The Austrians just wanted to declare war.

Nurse Jillian: What do you mean, Uncle?

Dr. John McCrae: Right after the incident, Austria sent a harsh ultimatum to Serbia. They blamed the Serbians for Ferdinand's death. Serbia did not want war. They wrote back, claiming that the government was innocent. The letter said that a private citizen had performed the assassination.

Nurse Jillian: So, what you are saying is that Serbia tried to cooperate with Austria, but it didn't matter.

Dr. John McCrae: You're right. Austria was bent on going to war. Supported by its German ally, Austria declared war on Serbia.

Nurse Jillian: That's terrible!

Dr. John McCrae: That's just the beginning, I'm afraid. Many countries in Europe have formed alliances with their friends. They have signed treaties promising to go to war for each other. Now, the different countries are acting on those promises and are beginning to declare war. Europe is on the brink of disaster. At this point, things look very bleak. It looks like we will soon be in the war ourselves.

Nurse Jillian: That's ridiculous! Canada is so far from Europe. Why would we have to go to war because of Ferdinand's death in Serbia? How did this happen?

Dr. John McCrae: Think of it as a raging fire that quickly got out of control. Once Germany and Austria declared war, they sent in troops to fight Serbia. Then, Russia sent in troops to protect Serbia. This made Germany and Austria angry. They told Russia to stop. Russia said it would not. So, Germany and Austria declared war against Russia.

Nurse Jillian: But, what does that have to do with us? I still don't understand.

Dr. John McCrae: Remember what I said about the treaties between countries? France signed a treaty to fight with Russia. So, Germany and Austria declared war against France, too, and now France has asked England to join them.

Nurse Jillian: Did England sign a treaty with France? Has England promised to join the war?

Dr. John McCrae: England hasn't signed a treaty, so it doesn't have to join France. But, something just happened that changes everything.

Nurse Jillian: What is that?

Dr. John McCrae: Germany just attacked Belgium, and Belgium does not belong to any alliances. It is a neutral country. This has made England angry. I guess England thinks that it can be attacked, too. So, today, England agreed to join the war effort against Austria and Germany.

Nurse Jillian: What does that mean for us?

Dr. John McCrae: It is bad news, Jillian. Canada is a dominion of the British Empire. When Britain is at war, Canada is also at war.

Nurse Jillian: What do you think will happen?

Dr. John McCrae: It's not what I think will happen. It's what I know will happen. With so many countries fighting in Europe, it will be a long and dangerous war.

Nurse Jillian: You are frightening me, Uncle.

Dr. John McCrae: I don't mean to frighten you, but a great number of our people will be sent to fight. I'm afraid that many of them will be wounded or killed. I made an important decision today, Jillian. It is a decision I knew might upset you, but I had to do it.

Nurse Jillian: What did you decide to do?

Dr. John McCrae: I don't feel right working at a hospital here when many Canadians will be asked to sacrifice their lives over there. I have a duty to my country and my country needs me now. I have decided to join the war effort. Today, I enlisted. As a doctor, I feel that I will be able to help save people on the battlefield. I hope you understand and won't argue.

Nurse Jillian: Argue with you, Uncle? No, I'm actually moved by what you've said, and as always, I think you did the right thing. I can't stand to think of our countrymen wounded and dying in foreign lands. In fact, I'm sure that they'll need nurses for the wounded soldiers. I think I will follow you, Uncle, and enlist as well.

Dr. John McCrae: No, Jillian, I'm not going to let you risk your life. You could get wounded, or worse.

Nurse Jillian: Uncle, I can't stay behind while this is happening. Don't I have a duty to my country as well?

Dr. John McCrae: Jillian, please don't do this.

Nurse Jillian: As a nurse, I have taken an oath to save lives.

Dr. John McCrae: You can keep your oath and still save lives in this hospital. It is far too dangerous for you. I have been assigned to the First Brigade in the Canadian Forces Artillery. My job will be to head a field hospital in Belgium in a place called Ypres. This is a place where great and terrible battles are being fought.

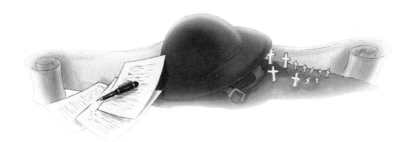

Nurse Jillian: Please don't try to dissuade me further, Uncle. My mind is made up. Our country needs both of us. Let's not argue because it will just drain the strength we need for the mission before us. I'm determined to join the war effort. I will follow your lead.

Dr. John McCrae: Well, if you insist on joining, I will go to the recruiting station with you. I will request that you be assigned as one of my nurses. That way, even if I can't protect you, at least I will be there with you.

Song: The Boys Who Fight for Freedom

Act 2

Alexis Helmer: Did you ever see so many wounded people? There are thousands of soldiers here. They all cry out for help. We can't fit all of them into the hospital. It's almost impossible to keep up.

Cyril Allinson: The sounds here are frightening! There is the constant sound of gunfire outside, and the piercing screams in here are unnerving. It's sad to watch so many soldiers gasping for air. I think it's because of the poison chlorine gas that the Germans are using. It is a terrible thing.

Alexis Helmer: This gas destroys people's lungs so they cannot get enough air. It is horrifying to watch the soldiers choke, especially when there is so little we can do to help them.

Cyril Allinson: So many of these soldiers will not make it.

Nurse Hathaway: All we can do is try to comfort them. I can't tell you how many times I have held the hand of a soldier as he died.

Cyril Allinson: There are more wounded men than we can handle. We don't have enough medical supplies, and we don't have enough beds.

Nurse Hathaway: But, what makes it so heartbreaking is that most of these soldiers know they won't make it.

Cyril Allinson: This is true. Even though we don't have enough staff, the staff we do have is completely devoted to the patients.

Nurse Hathaway: These soldiers are young and should have their whole lives ahead of them. They often cry when they talk of their sweethearts and their families at home. I do my best to listen because I don't want anybody to be alone when they die. But, sometimes the screams and agony of the other soldiers call me, and I have to leave their sides.

Alexis Helmer: If it weren't for Dr. McCrae, I'm not certain that I'd survive this. I get awfully scared sometimes. I just break down and cry to him. And as busy as he is, he always stops to listen.

Nurse Jillian: That's the way my uncle is. It's obvious that he is drained from all that is going on here. But, whenever he sees that one of us is down, he musters up his strength. He does everything he can to raise our spirits.

Alexis Helmer: To tell you the truth, he is my lifeline. I told him that yesterday, and he seemed touched. His encouragement is the only thing I am holding on to right now.

Cyril Allinson: I know this is grueling, but you are only 22, Alexis. You will find the strength, and you'll get through this.

Alexis Helmer: I hope what you are saying is true, but I just don't know. My home and my fiancée seem so far away now. I have a constant, nagging feeling that I will never see them again.

Cyril Allinson: Alexis, I know it's hard to witness all of this suffering and to not be able to help all of the wounded men here. But, you are strong. Someday you will be home with your family. Then, all of this will seem like a distant memory.

Alexis Helmer: All I can say is, I hope you are right.

Nurse Hathaway: Listen, everyone! Do you hear that strange, high-pitched whimpering? Look, there's a new soldier over there. Oh no, do you see his leg? Do you see what's happened to him? He's in agony! I must go to him immediately!

Alexis Helmer: I'll go with you, Anne. Maybe together we can help.

Cyril Allinson: There is another soldier in need over there. I will see both of you later.

Robert Smith: I've been shot, and I'm bleeding! Help me!

Nurse Hathaway: Hold on, soldier. Try to stay calm. We're here now, and I promise we'll do everything we can to take care of you. Here, hold this cloth tightly over the wound. You're losing a lot of blood, and it will help stop the bleeding.

Robert Smith: Thank you. Thank you so much.

Alexis Helmer: What is your name, and what happened to you?

Robert Smith: I am Private Robert Smith of the First Brigade. I heard an awful noise about a half hour ago, down a couple hundred yards from here at the headquarters of the infantry regiment. Then, I heard more shots. Some of the soldiers near me ducked while others ran, and the next thing I knew, I was hit. I couldn't get up and was losing a lot of blood, but there was no one to help me.

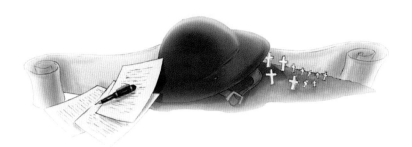

Nurse Hathaway: How did you get here with no one to help you?

Robert Smith: I crawled the whole way here. My leg was throbbing, so I had to slowly inch along. I didn't think I would make it. Whenever I heard gunfire, I crouched down and waited for the shooting to stop. It was agonizing and took a long time, but here I am.

Alexis Helmer: I see Dr. McCrae standing over there. Nurse Hathaway, could you ask him to come right away to get this bullet out? Please hurry. I don't want this soldier losing any more blood.

Nurse Hathaway: I'll hurry. I understand.

Alexis Helmer: Meanwhile, Private Smith, keep pressure on the wound with the cloth while I clean it.

Robert Smith: Will I get through this? I'm scared.

Alexis Helmer: Private Smith, you'll need to hold on and be very brave. I'm not sure if we have any anesthesia left. When Dr. McCrae operates to remove the bullet, we'll use a bit of whiskey. That will dull the pain. You will make it through this.

Robert Smith: Thank you for your help.

Alexis Helmer: We stayed with Robert Smith through most of the night. Like everyone else, he talked to us about his life, and we listened closely. He came from a military family in Canada and enlisted as soon as war broke out. The whiskey didn't really dull the pain, but Robert was courageous. All we could offer were words of comfort. I prayed he would make it through.

Robert Smith: I'm frightened, and I need you to promise you will do something for me. I have a letter in my pocket that I want my family to have if I don't get through the night. I want them to know that I love them. Will you promise to send it to them?

Nurse Hathaway: Of course we will, Robert, but I promise that you will make it through this. Don't worry, we'll stay here with you, and we'll see to that!

Robert Smith: I pray that you're right. I'm only 18, and I'm not ready to die.

Nurse Hathaway: Would you like me to hold your hand, Robert?

Robert Smith: Thank you, Nurse, it would mean a lot to me. Then, maybe I won't feel so alone.

Nurse Hathaway: It was a grueling night. I could see that Dr. McCrae was just as worried about Alexis as he was about the wounded soldier.

Dr. John McCrae: There was something remarkable about Alexis. We had been at this field hospital for 17 days and 17 nights, and none of us had changed clothes or taken off our boots.

Alexis Helmer: I don't think I had ever slept more than a few minutes at a time. I never wanted to leave a patient's side.

Dr. John McCrae: I felt close to my staff. We depended on each other. But Alexis, even more than the others, gave everything he had. Then he said a simple thing to me that finally gave me the excuse I needed to send him off to the dugout.

Alexis Helmer: I'm relieved that Robert has finally fallen asleep. Dr. McCrae, just listen. It's a little quieter here now. I don't hear any gunfire. It almost seems peaceful. Don't you think so?

Dr. John McCrae: Yes, Alexis, I do. And, I do not need your help right now. You must try to get a good night's sleep.

Alexis Helmer: If you are sure there is nothing else I can do, sir, I will. Thank you.

Dr. John McCrae: And then, Alexis repeated the words to me, as if for the last time.

Alexis Helmer: It has quieted a little, and I shall try to get some sleep.

Act 3

Cyril Allinson: The events of Sunday, the second of May, 1915, have left all of us in a state of shock. Early this morning, Alexis Helmer left his dugout to check on a wounded soldier. He managed to get only a few yards from the dugout when it happened. A German shell struck him. The shell burst, and Alexis was killed instantly.

Nurse Hathaway: His scattered remains were gathered in an army blanket for burial that evening.

Cyril Allinson: On his body we found a picture of his fiancée. It had a hole right through it. We decided to bury it with him.

Nurse Hathaway: His burial was in the cemetery right next to the hospital. We called it Flanders Fields. Sometimes in the morning we could hear the larks singing during the brief silences between the bursts of the shells. It was strange when we did.

Cyril Allinson: We had watched that cemetery grow for the last 17 days. Even when there was only a 10-minute lull in the fighting, we would see it happen. Soldiers from the nearby infantry unit would creep silently in to bury their dead. Day by day it grew, and soon there were rows and rows of simple white crosses. Alexis's cross would soon be added to the rest.

Nurse Hathaway: There was no chaplain, so Dr. McCrae said he'd perform the funeral ceremony himself.

Cyril Allinson: Dr. McCrae barely spoke to any of us. He was too overcome with grief. I wasn't sure he would be able to perform the ceremony. But when the time came, he recited some of the passages he remembered from the Church of England's "Order of Burial of the Dead."

Dr. John McCrae: "We brought nothing into this world, and it is certain we can carry nothing out. The Lord gave, and the Lord hath taken away; blessed be the name of the Lord."

Act 4

Nurse Jillian: I'm very worried about my uncle. He's heartbroken and totally silent; I've never seen him like this. When I made an attempt to talk to him earlier, he wouldn't even look at me. It was like he was walking in a dream. I didn't know how to comfort him, and I don't even know where he is now.

Cyril Allinson: I saw him sitting on the ambulance earlier. He had paper, and he seemed to be writing something. He kept looking back and forth, over and over at Alexis's grave, and then writing on the paper. It was almost like he was in a trance. I didn't speak to him at all.

Nurse Hathaway: I watched him for a little while, too, and I know what you are saying. Sometimes, he would just stop and stare at the poppies blowing softly in the breeze by the grave markings.

Cyril Allinson: Look over there. There's one bit of good news this morning. Robert Smith has not just survived, he's actually walking around. Why, he's coming here now.

Robert Smith: Have any of you seen Dr. McCrae? I wanted to thank him myself. I really didn't expect to wake up again after he removed the bullet, and I can't believe I am walking again. I also wanted to thank that young soldier who stayed with me. I think his name was Alexis.

Cyril Allinson: I'm afraid you can't do that, soldier. Alexis was killed yesterday, and Dr. McCrae is very upset. Look, I see him now. He's way over there by the ambulance.

Robert Smith: I'm so sorry to hear about Alexis. Maybe I can speak to Dr. McCrae later.

Nurse Hathaway: Wait a minute; I think Dr. McCrae is getting up now. Robert, you may get your chance to thank Dr. McCrae. Look, he's walking in this direction.

Cyril Allinson: Dr. McCrae, are you okay? Is there anything we can do for you?

Dr. John McCrae: I'm glad you are all here because I have something I need to show you. But before I do, I want to ask the questions that have haunted me. When we enlisted, I don't think any of us had even the slightest idea of the horrors we would witness. We have all made great sacrifices and have lost people we love. Do you think this war is worth those sacrifices? Do you think the world will be a better place because of this war?

Robert Smith: When I enlisted, my father told me something, and I think about what he said every day. He told me that this was the war that would end all wars. That is why I wanted to be a part of it. I wanted to be in the war that would finally bring peace for all time.

Cyril Allinson: Do you still believe that, soldier?

Robert Smith: I know that what we have been through has been terrible and that none of us will ever be the same. But, I believe what my father said, more than ever. I don't think that the sacrifices we or our countrymen have made were in vain.

Dr. John McCrae: Let us pray, Private Smith, that you are right. I want to show all of you the poem I just wrote. I wrote it in memory of Alexis Helmer. I wrote it to honor the memory of all the valiant soldiers who have sacrificed everything in this Great War. Now all we can do is pray that this is, indeed, the war to end all wars.

Poem: In Flanders Fields

In Flanders Fields

by Lieutenant Colonel John McCrae, M.D.
Canadian Army

In Flanders Fields the poppies blow
Between the crosses row on row
That mark our place; and in the sky
The larks, still bravely singing, fly
Scarce heard amid the guns below.

We are the Dead. Short days ago
We lived, felt dawn, saw sunset glow,
Loved and were loved, and now we lie
In Flanders Fields.

Take up our quarrel with the foe:
To you from failing hands we throw
The torch; be yours to hold it high.
If ye break faith with us who die
We shall not sleep, though poppies grow
In Flanders Fields.

The Boys Who Fight for Freedom

by Anonymous

Bugle calls are sounding, sounding ev'rywhere.
Britain's boys are 'listing, boys we love so dear.
Joining Britain's army, going across the sea,
To strike a blow for freedom's sake and win a victory.

For the boys who love a land of freedom
Are the boys who fight for Britain's name,
And we'll give them all a hearty welcome
When they return again.

Boys who love their country, boys of splendid frame,
Side by side are fighting, fighting might and main.
They don't mind the danger on land or on the sea
So long as they can win the fight, the fight for liberty.

This is an abridged version of the complete song.

Glossary

alliance — an agreement between two or more countries in which they promise to help one another

battalion — a unit of people in the military, usually two to six companies; units have 500–1,500 people and are commanded by a lieutenant colonel

brigade — a large group of troops

chaplain — a person who conducts religious ceremonies in the military

dominion — a former colony, like Canada, that was under foreign rule but was also ruled by its own independent government

dugout — a shelter dug in a hillside

enlist — to join voluntarily

Hades — in ancient Greek mythology, the underworld where the dead live

infantry — soldiers who usually fight with small weapons but may be trained to fight with advanced weapon systems, as well

neutral — not taking sides

regiment — a military unit that includes more than one battalion; regiments are commanded by a colonel

ultimatum — a demand that must be met at a specific time; if the demand is not met, then the party receiving the ultimatum could be punished